Published in Great Britain in 1988 by World International Publishing Limited,
An Egmont Company, Egmont House, P.O. Box 111,
Great Ducie Street, Manchester M60 3BL.
Printed in Hungary. ISBN 7235 1111 X

# Enid Blyton's

# TELL-A-STORY BOOK

## Clever-One the Imp
## and other stories

# Pull, Mr. Stamp-About, Pull!

ONE day little Mr. Plump went shopping with his big shopping-basket. He shouldn't have taken that basket because the bottom of it was falling to pieces, as Mrs. Plump had often told him.

But he forgot, and took it along to the shops. He bought a nice currant cake at the baker's. He bought a bunch of carrots at the greengrocer's. He bought a box of chocolates at the sweet-shop.

Then he went to the butcher, and got the Sunday joint. He didn't notice that the bottom was falling out of his basket. Bump! The cake fell out. Thud! Down went the carrots! Bump! That was the nice little box of chocolates.

The joint was too big to fall out. Mr. Plump didn't notice his goods dropping on to the path. He saw the joint in the basket, and thought that the other things were underneath.

But somebody else noticed the things falling out! That was Mr. Stamp-About, who happened to be walking just behind Mr. Plump when the cake dropped out.

He guessed what was happening at once! Aha! There was a hole in Mr. Plump's basket!

Now most people would at once have run after Mr. Plump and told him what was happening. But not Mr. Stamp-About. Oh, no. He just picked up the cake and popped it into his own basket. Then he waited for the next thing to drop. Hurrah! Carrots! They went into his basket, too. And the box of chocolates followed them.

Little Mrs. Trot saw what Mr. Stamp-About was doing, and she was upset. She was afraid of Mr. Stamp-About, because he had a very bad temper, but she thought she really must tell poor Mr. Plump.

So she hurried up to him and whispered: "Mr. Plump! You are dropping things out of your basket, and Mr. Stamp-About has picked them up and put them into his!"

Mr. Plump stopped and looked into his basket. Good gracious! There was only the joint there. He glared at Mr. Stamp-About.

"Have you picked up my goods?" he said.

"Certainly not," said Mr. Stamp-About most untruthfully.

Mr. Plump looked into Mr. Stamp-About's basket, and there he saw all his lost goods. He pointed at them. "You are a thief, Mr. Stamp-About. Give me them back at once, or I will fight you!"

"Pooh! I am stronger than you," said Mr. Stamp-About, scornfully.

"You're not!"

"I am! You're big and fat, but you're not strong like me," said Mr. Stamp-About.

Then an idea came into Mr. Plump's head. "Let's prove who is the stronger of us two! I've got

a rope here, see? I'll go round this corner, and you stay here, and pull hard. If you can pull me round the corner, you can keep my goods. If you can't, I'll have them back!"

"Right!" said Mr. Stamp-About, who was quite certain he could pull Mr. Plump round the corner at once. He took one end of the rope, and Mr. Plump took the other and disappeared round the corner.

A crowd began to gather. "I'll tell you when to pull," said Jinky, Mr. Plump's friend. He peeped round the corner at Mr. Plump and grinned. He felt certain that Mr. Plump was up to something!

So he was. He was busy tying his end of the rope to a lamp-post. Ha! Pull, Mr. Stamp-About, pull all you like!

"Now—one, two, three, PULL!" yelled Jinky. And Mr. Stamp-About pulled. My, how he pulled! He breathed hard, and he pulled till he went purple in the face.

Everyone yelled to him. "Pull, Mr. Stamp-About, pull! Pull hard! Go on, Mr. Stamp-About, PULL, PULL, PULL!"

And Mr. Stamp-About pulled till his arms nearly came out. But although the lamp-post moved about half an inch, it wouldn't move any more—and as for Mr. Plump, he wasn't there at all!

No—he had run all the way round the next corner, and the next, and lo and behold! there he was round the third corner, just behind Mr. Stamp-About, who was pulling for all he was worth. Behind him was his basket, full of Mr. Plump's dropped goods. Mr. Plump saw it, snatched it up, and ran off home with it, his basket of meat in the other hand. The crowd saw him, and laughed, for little Mrs. Trot had told them all about it.

"Pull, Mr. Stamp-About, pull!" yelled everyone. "You're not as strong as you thought you were. Pull! Pull! Pull!"

Mr. Stamp-About was angry. How dare Mr. Plump pull against him so hard? He gave a jerk at the rope and the lamp-post moved a little. Mr. Stamp-About gave another jerk, and dear me, the lamp-post shook and shivered.

"He's coming!" said Mr. Stamp-About, pleased. "Aha, Mr. Plump is coming! He'll soon be round the corner at a run—and then I'll pull his nose for him!"

He gave a simply enormous tug at the rope and the lamp-post came out of the ground with a crash. Mr. Plod the policeman, who happened to be walking just on the opposite side of the road, was very startled to see the lamp-post jump out of the ground and then crash down.

"What's all this?" he said to himself. Then he saw that a rope was tied to it. "My goodness me—somebody is actually pulling lamp-posts up!"

He went round the corner at a run, and Mr. Stamp-About, who had expected to see Mr. Plump coming, was most astonished to see the policeman instead.

"Ah, Mr. Stamp-About, so it's you, is it, pulling lamp-posts up!" roared Mr. Plod angrily. "How dare you? Are you mad? Tying ropes to lamp-posts and yanking them up like that! You come along with me!"

"I didn't tie ropes round a lamp-post!" said Mr. Stamp-About, indignantly. "I tell you I didn't."

"Well, I don't care who did the rope-tying. It's you that is doing the pulling," said Mr. Plod.

"But—but—I wasn't pulling at a lamp-post, I was pulling at Mr. Plump," said Mr. Stamp-About.

"Story-teller! I saw Mr. Plump going into his cottage a few minutes ago with his shopping," said

12

Mr. Plod. "Do you want me to tie *you* up with that rope, Mr. Stamp-About? If you don't come along with me, I will!"

"B-b-b-but—" began Mr. Stamp-About again, more puzzled than ever. Mr. Plod didn't want to listen to any more.

"Stop your butting, or I'll think you're a goat," he said. "Come along! You'll have to pay for that lamp-post to be mended and put back again."

"Where's my basket?" said Mr. Stamp-About, looking round. "Where's my *basket*?"

Nobody said a word. But everyone grinned and Jinky let out a great big haw-haw-haw. Mr. Stamp-About lost his temper. He stamped and he raged, till Mr. Plod took hold of his coat collar and marched him quickly off to the police-station.

As for Mr. Plump, he didn't go near Mr. Stamp-About for a long time—and how he laughed when Jinky told him that Mr. Stamp-About had had to pay for the lamp-post. It really served old Stamp-About right, didn't it?

# Tick-Tock, Tick-Tock

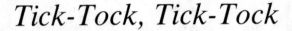

TICK-TOCK, tick-tock,
I'm the little kitchen clock.

Tickety-tock, tockety-tick,
I'm a watch and I'm very quick.

TICK-TOCK-TICK-TOCK,
I'm the old grandfather clock.

Ding-dong-ding-dong,
I'm the church clock, big and
   strong,
Chiming through the day and
   night,
Keeping time with all my might.

Tick-tock, tick-tock,
Tickety-tock, tockety-tick,
TICK-TOCK-TICK-
   TOCK,
DING-DONG-DING-
   DONG.

# The Boy On The Bicycle

MOTHER was telling the two children what to buy that morning She was ill in bed, so she couldn't do any shopping or work.

Jane had cleaned up the little house as best she could, and Will had brought in some wood and coal for the fire. Now they were to go and do the shopping.

Jane looked down at the list of things. "I wish we could buy some eggs for you and some fruit, Mother," she said. "The doctor said you were to have them, you know. But you haven't put them down on the list."

"There isn't money enough for them, dear," said Mother. "So I must do without. I'm lucky to have two children like you that I can trust. I'd rather have that than eggs and fruit."

15

"I'd like you to have *both*," said Will. He fetched the basket and the two set off to the town. It was Saturday morning and very busy. Cars swept by, and errand boys on bicycles darted here and there.

Suddenly there came a cry. "Look out, there! You'll have an accident!"

The two children looked round. Down the hill came a boy on a bicycle at top speed. He seemed to have forgotten that he had any brakes to put on. He swung round the corner by Jane without putting his hand out to warn traffic. A car pulled up quickly and almost ran on to the pavement.

The boy fell off his bicycle, sat up on the road and howled. He had bruised his arm, grazed his hands and hurt his knees.

Will picked up his bicycle, which had the front wheel bent. Jane picked up the boy and dusted him down. People came round to see if he was all right, but finding that two children were seeing to him, and that he wasn't much hurt, they went away again. But the man in the car called out crossly: "Don't you come out on your bike again till you've learnt the rules of the road."

The boy was still crying. "Cheer up," said Will. "You're not much hurt. We'll take you home, if you like. Where do you live?"

"At the big house," said the boy, pointing up the hill. " We've only just come, about two weeks ago. Oh, my poor knee!"

"It just wants bathing," said Jane. "Come along up the hill. Will can wheel your bike. Your mother can bathe your knee and bandage it."

"I want you to bathe my knee," said the boy. "My name's Mike. What's yours?"

Wiping away his tears, the boy walked up the hill with Jane and Will, telling them about his new house and the lovely garden.

"There are peaches in the greenhouse," he said. "And plums on the trees all purple and ripe. And we are going to have thousands of apples and pears."

"You're lucky," said Jane. "We have just one fruit tree in our garden, and that's an apple tree that never has any apples!"

They turned in at a big gateway and walked up the drive. It was so big that Jane felt rather scared.

17

"I don't think we'd better come any farther," she said.

"Yes, come to my play-room," said Mike. "You said you'd bathe my knee for me. I don't want my mother to."

"Why not?" said Jane. "I always like my mother to see to me if I'm hurt."

They came to a big play-room with a garden door. They went in. There was a basin with hot and cold water at one end, and Jane went to it. She found a flannel and began to bathe Mike's knee gently.

Mike began to boast. "Did you see me come down the hill at top speed? I'm not allowed to go out of the garden, really! Not till I'm more used to my bike. I've only had it three days. Mother said I wasn't to go into the village yet."

Jane stopped bathing Mike's knee. She looked up at him.

"Well, your mother was quite right. See what a nasty little accident you had! You came down that hill without even putting your brakes on. You might have fallen right under that car. Your mother will be upset when she hears."

"She won't hear," said Mike. "I shan't tell her. She'll think I fell off my bike in the garden. I keep lots of things from my mother."

"Then I think you deserve to have an accident," said Will, in disgust. "Here you've got a lovely house and a gorgeous garden, and a new bike, and

a sensible, kind mother—and you go off and disobey her and then say you're going to deceive her. Come on, Jane. Don't bother about his knee. He's not worth bringing home and making a fuss about!"

There was a movement at the end of the room and a man came forward. It was Mike's father. He had been there all the time!

"I was watching you two kind children," he said, "and I couldn't help hearing all you said. You are quite right to talk to Mike like that. He needs friends like you! He's a spoilt, disobedient little boy, who doesn't know how lucky he is."

"Well—he is lucky," said Jane, going red. "We've only got a little cottage—and our mother is ill, and we can't even get her the eggs and fruit the doctor says she ought to have. We're looking after her as best we can. We wouldn't dream of being silly like Mike, and upsetting her by having an accident because we were stupid and deceitful."

"You hear that, Mike?" said his father. "Now you see what sensible, good-hearted children think of you when you boast of being disobedient and deceitful. I hope you're ashamed of yourself. These are the sort of children who would make very fine friends for you—but I'm sure that now they won't want to see you again."

Mike looked as if he was going to burst into tears again. He caught hold of Jane's hand. "I was just boasting," he said. "I'd look after my mother, too, if she was ill. I'm sorry about yours. Daddy, can I get some eggs from the hen-house and some peaches and plums and take them to Jane's mother? And, please, Jane and Will, come and see me again. I haven't got any friends here."

20

Jane was delighted to hear about the eggs and the fruit. Just what Mother ought to have. She smiled at Mike. "Perhaps you're not so bad as you sound," she said. "If your father likes, we *will* come and see you again, and play with you."

"And put a bit of your commonsense and kindness into his head," said Mike's father. "I'd like you to do that. Come along; we'll get the eggs. And when your mother can spare you, come and play with Mike, and stay to tea."

That was how Jane and Will bcame friends with Mike, up at the big house. Mike learnt a lot from them, and in return he gave them the eggs and fruit their mother needed, so that she soon got better.

Will has taught him the rules of the road and now Mike is allowed to go out on his bicycle by himself into the town. Very often he lends it to Will and Jane—and how grand they feel pedalling along to do the shopping!

They don't know it yet, but Mike's father and mother are giving them bicycles on their next birthdays. Won't it be a fine surprise!

# A Traffic Puzzle

In this busy road you'll see
Things that start with Letter C.

Now see if you can quickly tell
What begins with Letter L.

Two things start with Letter B
And one begins with Letter T.

With Letter M two more begin,
And make a really dreadful din.

And Letter H you'll find is there,
Belonging to a handsome pair.

22

23

# Clever-One The Imp

AT one end of Tick-Tock Village lived the goblin, Gloomy. At the other end lived the witch, Greedy. In between were the cottages of the pixies, elves and imps.

"We're most unlucky," they said to one another when they met at the market each day. "If we don't meet Gloomy, with his bad temper and moans and groans, we bump into Greedy, with her horrid ways. And we don't dare to offend them because they really know more magic than we do!"

Clever-One the imp didn't know Gloomy or Greedy. He had just come to stay with his brother, Poppit, who lived near to Gloomy. He listened to everything that was said, and then he looked very thoughtful.

Poppit looked at him. "He's thinking very hard.

24

Soon his head will swell up and we shall know he's got a good idea."

Just then Greedy came by and pushed everyone out of the way. Then Gloomy came up, frowning and muttering, and all the little folk scurried off. But not Clever-One. He still stayed where he was, thinking. His head swelled up and Poppit, who was watching him from a good way off, knew that he had suddenly got an idea.

Greedy glared at him and pushed him off the pavement. Gloomy, who was walking in the road, bumped into him, and pushed him back onto the pavement.

"What are you dreaming of?" he growled. "Standing there in everybody's way."

"Dear me, I'm so sorry," said Clever-One, "but the truth is, I was just wondering where in the world I put the magic broomstick that belonged to my grandmother. It would be so useful just now, because my car has broken down. It's a wonderful broomstick, better than any other in the world, because it goes higher and faster."

Gloomy and Greedy stared at Clever-One and suddenly became quite polite to him. "What a wonderful broomstick!" said Witch Greedy, who only had a very ordinary one that refused to fly at all on a rainy or a windy night.

"Where *can* it be?" said Goblin Gloomy, who hadn't got a flyaway broomstick at all.

"I must find out," said Clever-One. "Yes, I

really must. I'll hunt for it till I find it."

"*Do* let me know when you find it," said Greedy. "I'll buy it from you."

"No. I'll buy it!" said Gloomy, crossly. "She's got one already. Greedy thing!"

"I'll make your nose grow long and then put a knot in it!" said Witch Greedy, angrily.

Goodness knows what would have happened if Clever-One hadn't walked off, still looking as if he was thinking very deeply. The goblin and the witch both followed him at once. They kept him in sight all day and he led them a fine dance. But when night came, and all three were tired, Clever-One made his way to a lonely cave in a hill at the back of the village. Gloomy and Greedy followed him, feeling certain that the imp had remembered the place where his grandmother's broomstick was.

In the cave, sure enough, was a long, strong broomstick, with a fine sweeping-end that had never been used. "Aha!" said Clever-One, loudly. "Here it is." He took hold of it, sat on the stick and galloped round the cave with it.

Greedy and Gloomy both rushed in. They caught hold of the broomstick too. "Sell it to me!" cried Gloomy. "No, to me!" shouted Greedy, and they both tried to tug it away.

"Now, now, what manners!" said Clever-One, shocked. "Surely you don't want to break it between you? Now, I'll tell you what I'll do. I'll let you each have a ride on it to see if you like it

26

before you buy it."

"No," said Greedy. "If Gloomy sits on it and rides off, he'll never come back. I know him, the deceitful rogue."

"Ho!" said Gloomy, frowning so hard that his eyes disappeared. "And what about *you*, madam? I know perfectly well that once *you* get on it, you'll ride off through the night, and keep the stick for your own for always."

"Dear, dear!" said Clever-One, looking puzzled. "Then I daren't let either of you ride alone. I know! You can take a ride together! That will be a splendid idea."

27

Greedy and Gloomy looked sharply at Clever-One. "There's a trick in this!" said Gloomy. "I smell it! You're going to send us both off somewhere on this magic broomstick of yours —and you think we'll never come back, so that the Village of Tick-Tock will be rid of us!"

"Very well," said Clever-One, looking offended. "If you think that, don't ride the broomstick. I'll have it for myself."

"No. You ride with us!" cried Greedy, and pulled Clever-One down on to the broomstick in front of her. "Get on, Gloomy. Now, if he plays any tricks with us, and sends us off to the moon, he'll go too! Ha, ha, ha!"

"Wait, wait! Let me strap my parcel on my back," said Clever-One and picked up something from the floor. He put it over his shoulders. "I need both hands to hold on to the broomstick."

All three sat on the big broomstick, and walked it to the cave entrance. Clever-One suddenly struck the stick hard and cried out loudly. "To the Moon! To the Moon! And don't come back, old broomstick!"

"You rogue!" cried the witch. "I thought you'd play a trick. But you'll have to come too! Ho, ho! We shall make you our servant up there, and lead you an awful life!"

Up into the air went the broomstick with a loud swishing noise like a rocket. The three held on tightly. The broomstick circled round and then went straight up towards the big round moon in the sky.

Was Clever-One frightened? Did he mind what was happening? Not a bit of it!

When they were fairly high up, just reaching the first clouds, Clever-One pulled a cord that hung down in front of him, and was attached to the parcel he carried. Then he suddenly leapt off the broomstick, with such a terrible yell that the witch and the goblin almost fell off in fright themselves.

"He's gone!" said Gloomy. "Good riddance! That's the end of him!"

"He'll never play tricks on anyone again," said Greedy. "Nasty little imp! Serves him right."

But it wasn't the end of Clever-One. Oh, no! The parcel he had tied to himself was a neatly folded parachute, and when he pulled the cord, and jumped off into the air, the parachute began to open! Soon it was fully open, and Clever-One began to float gently downwards to earth.

"Here I come!" he shouted to all the folk of Tick-Tock, who had heard the swishing of the broomstick and had come running out to see what was happening. "Here I come! I'm frozen. Somebody get me some hot cocoa!"

"Where are Greedy and Gloomy?" cried Poppit.

"On the cold, cold moon, I hope," said Clever-One, coming gently to earth. "They wanted my broomstick and they got it. We shall never see them again."

Wasn't he clever? He drank six cups of hot cocoa, and really he did deserve them!

1. Here are two gollys playing with an engine. Write down the first letter of the three things shown. Sort them out, put them in the right order, and find something you like for breakfast!

2. Here is an imp sharing an apple and a nut with a rabbit. Write down the first letter of each, sort them out, put them in the right order, and find something that all flowers love.

3. Here is an Armchair with a Brownie sitting in it, having his Tea. Write down the first letter of each, sort them out, put them in the right order, and find something that is useful in cricket!

4. Here are two pixies buying two eggs, an orange and a banana. Write down the first letter of each, sort them out, put them in the right order, and find the name of the girl in the Nursery Rhyme!

# She Couldn't Keep
# A Secret

IT wasn't a bit of good telling anything to Marybelle if you wanted to keep it secret—because Marybelle would at once go round and tell everyone else!

It was most annoying. When Kitty told Marybelle she was making a hanky-case for her friend Lucy, and it was to be a real surprise, what did Marybelle do but go and whisper it into Lucy's ear at once. So it wasn't a surprise after all.

And when Tom mentioned to Marybelle that his mother couldn't give him money that week to buy the toy he wanted, Marybelle ran round and told everyone that Tom's mother was so poor she couldn't even buy him a toy!

That made Tom very angry. He spoke to the

others when Marybelle wasn't there. "Can't we stop that silly Marybelle from repeating everything, and sometimes repeating it wrong?" he said. "She really does make such mischief—and she never gets punished for it!"

"Well, it's our own fault for telling her things," said Lucy.

"Yes, but you can't remember not to talk to Marybelle," said Tom. "I can't, anyway."

"I think I know how we could stop her running round and repeating everything," said Ronnie, with a grin.

"How?" asked everyone at once.

"Well," said Ronnie, "we could tell her silly, ridiculous things and beg her not to repeat them in case they aren't true—which they wouldn't be, of course. And then when she *does* go and repeat them everyone will laugh at her. She won't like that."

"What kind of things would we say?" asked Tom.

"Well—I could say, 'I say, Marybelle, have you heard that the postman lost all his letters in the duck-pond yesterday?'" said Ronnie. "And I would say, 'Now, don't tell anyone, because it probably isn't true.' But off she would go, of course, and what a to-do there would be!"

"Yes. That sounds a good idea," said Tom. "We'll do it. You tell her that one about the postman to start with, Ronnie."

So Ronnie did. He waited until he had got Marybelle alone, and then he whispered mysteriously to her, "Marybelle, have you heard that the postman lost all his letters in the duck-pond yesterday? Don't repeat it, for it may not be true."

Marybelle's eyes almost fell out of her head. Gracious! All the letters lost—in the duck-pond too!

She ran off at once. "Did you know that the postman dropped all the letters into the duck-pond yesterday?" she said to everyone she met. "Well, he did!"

Now, the postman's little boy heard that Marybelle was saying this, and he asked his father about it. The postman was most annoyed. He went straight to Marybelle's house and asked to see her mother.

"Will you please stop your little girl from saying that I dropped all the letters into the duck-pond yesterday?" he said. "I am most annoyed about it. I have never lost a letter in my life!"

Poor Marybelle! She had to apologise to the postman. She scolded Ronnie for saying such a thing.

"Well, I told you not to repeat it in case it wasn't true," said Ronnie. "It's your own fault." ·

Now the next day Tom went up to Marybelle and whispered something to her. "Have you heard that old Mrs. Loo, the sweetshop woman, gives peppermints to her hens, and that's why she never has any when we want to buy them?" he said. "Now, don't you repeat that, Marybelle, in case it isn't true."

"Gives peppermints to hens!" cried Marybelle. "The silly old woman! No wonder she has none to sell."

Off ran Marybelle to tell everyone. How they laughed at her behind her back! But somebody happened to tell old Mrs. Loo about it and she was very cross. And the next time Marybelle went into her shop for some sweets, she wouldn't sell her any.

"No," she said. "You're the silly girl that says I feed my hens with peppermints. Such a stupid thing to say! Why, I'd make them all ill if I did. You go away and buy sweets somewhere else."

Marybelle cried. She went to Tom and told him he was mean to tell her something that wasn't true. "Well, I warned you not to say anything, in case it wasn't true," said Tom. "It is your own fault, Marybelle."

36

Then Lucy had a turn. She went to Marybelle, looking most mysterious.

"Marybelle! Have you heard that the grocer has a pony he will let children ride up and down the street for a penny? Isn't it exciting? But don't say a word about it in case it isn't true."

Well, Marybelle loved riding ponies, and she made up her mind to be the first one riding the grocer's. So she took a penny from her money-box and ran to the shop.

"Please," she said to the grocer, "here is my penny. Now let me ride on your pony."

"What pony?" said the grocer.

"*Yours*!" said Marybelle. "I've heard that we can ride it for a penny."

"Don't be silly," said the grocer. "I've got no pony, and I wouldn't let you children ride it if I had. Run away and don't come to me with silly ideas like that."

How everyone laughed at Marybelle! She was very angry with Lucy. "Well, I told you it might not be true," said Lucy. "I did warn you, Marybelle."

Then Jack went to Marybelle, and told her a little story of his own. "Marybelle! Have you heard that Teacher's dog chased Mrs. Brown's cat, and bit its tail?" he said. "Now, don't you repeat that, in case it isn't true."

Any bit of news, however silly or small, was enough to set Marybelle's tongue wagging. In a trice she was telling everyone what Jack had said.

"I say, did you know that Teacher's dog chased Mrs. Brown's cat and bit its tail? Fancy that! Teacher always says her dog never chases cats."

Now, old Mrs. Brown was the great-aunt of one of the children. This child told Mrs. Brown what Marybelle had said, and she was full of horror to think that her poor cat had been chased and bitten by the teacher's big dog.

So up she went to the school to complain. "I shall go to the police about it if your dog chases my cat again," she said. "A great big dog like that!"

"But he *never* chases anything!" said the teacher, in surprise. "He's too old. Who told you that, Mrs. Brown?"

"My great-niece, young Gladys," said Mrs. Brown. So Gladys was sent for, and asked about the tale of the dog and the cat.

"Oh, Marybelle told me," said Gladys. "She was telling everyone."

Then Marybelle was sent for, and was well scolded by the teacher for saying such an unkind thing about her poor old dog.

"Jack told me," wept Marybelle.

"It was only a made-up story," said Jack, grinning. "I warned Marybelle not to repeat it in case it wasn't true. But she can't help repeating anything, however silly it is—or however secret. We've been stuffing her up with all sorts of silly tales, and she's been repeating them all—and getting into trouble, too!"

Marybelle burst into tears again. "You horrid boy! You've got me into trouble."

"No. You got yourself into trouble," said Jack. "And you always will, Marybelle. You can't hold your tongue, you see, and you can never keep a secret, even if it belongs to somebody else."

"Then I shan't ever believe anything anyone says!" said Marybelle, angrily.

"Right," said Jack. "Then, maybe, you won't repeat it!"

And now poor Marybelle is in a great fix, because she never knows whether any bit of news is true or made-up. So she doesn't dare to repeat it in case she gets into trouble again.

It's a funny way of learning to keep secrets, isn't it? But it's the only way with the Marybelles!

### ANSWERS TO TRAFFIC PUZZLE

Car, Caravan, Coach—Lorry—Bus, Bicycle, Tram—Motor-bikes (two)—Horses (two).

### ANSWER TO RIDDLE-ME-REE

School

# Tweaky's Trick

THERE was once a small goblin called Tweaky, who made a bargain with the thrushes.

"I am small enough to pop down the worm-holes and tweak the worms out for you to eat," said Tweaky slyly to the thrushes. "What will you give me if I do?"

"We'll give you feathers to make yourself a warm, winter coat," said the thrushes.

"Oh, good!" said Tweaky, pleased, for he felt the cold very much in the winter. "But give me the small freckled feathers off your chests, please—they will be the warmest for me."

Now this bargain pleased the thrushes and it pleased the goblin too—but it didn't please the worms at all!

"It is hard enough to escape the birds as it is, without being pulled out of our holes for them," said one worm.

"If I hadn't held on to the end of my hole very

41

tightly indeed, Tweaky would have had me right out yesterday," said another. "It's too bad."

"He slips down our holes and pulls us before we know he is there," said a third worm. "Do you know, he pulled seven worms out this morning, and the thrushes gobbled them all up at once. They hadn't a chance to get away."

"It's time he was stopped," said the first worm.

But nobody knew how to stop Tweaky, and every morning early he popped down the worm-holes and managed to pull up a few worms for the thrushes. And in return they gave him a small feather for each worm.

"I shall soon have enough feathers to make myself a lovely, warm, winter coat!" cried Tweaky. He stored the feathers in an empty worm-hole. He was very pleased with them.

Now the worms soon saw that unless something was done to stop the goblin from tweaking them out of their holes, there would be no worms left. So they sent to the elf, Kindly, to help them.

Kindly was a small creature, as nice as her name. She listened in surprise to the worms' story.

"Tweaky shouldn't do a thing like that," she said. "No fairy creature is allowed to bring harm to any flower, tree, bird, insect or animal. It is very wrong of him. But I daren't try to stop him, for he is a spiteful little creature."

"What shall we do, then?" said the poor worms unhappily.

"Wait a minute," said Kindly, thinking hard. "I may be able to help you in some way. Ah, yes! I have a good idea! Why don't you stuff up your holes each night, then he can't squeeze down them to catch you?"

"That seems a good idea," said the worms. "But what can we stuff up our holes with?"

"I'll soon find something," said Kindly, and she hurried off. It was autumn-time, and there were leaves on the ground. There were pine-needles too. There were bits of straw and stick—quite a lot of things that would be useful for stuffing up holes!

Kindly collected a great many. "Go into your holes!" she said to the worms. "I'll see what I can do to stuff them up for you."

So they all went into their holes and Kindly stuffed up the entrances with the dead leaves, the pine-needles and the bits of straw and tiny sticks.

"Are you all right?" she called.

"Fine!" answered the worms in delight. "Oh, Kindly, we do feel so warm, too! The frost and the

wind can't make us shiver in our holes now! We are as cosy as can be!"

Well, when Tweaky came along the next morning to catch the worms and pull them from their holes, he found them all stuffed up, so that he couldn't squeeze down them. He was very angry. The thrushes wouldn't give him any feathers because he had no worms for them.

"This is a fine idea, Kindly," said the worms in delight. "Will you do this for us always?"

"No, I can't," said Kindly. "I am going away soon for a month. I must teach you to stuff up your holes for yourselves."

So she taught them how to find the leaves and pine-needles and other odds and ends, and they soon learnt how to stuff up their holes nicely. They even learnt the right way to pull the pine-needles into their holes—by the joined end, for then they slipped in well, but they wouldn't go in properly if they pulled them in by the wrong end!

"You are quite clever," said Kindly, pleased.

44

"Now I'm going, so goodbye. Look after yourselves well, and you will be quite safe."

So they did. Every night they hunted for something to stuff up their holes, and always they pulled in the pine-needles by the right end. In the mornings Tweaky could never get into their holes, and he soon gave it up. One of the worms found his store of feathers, and used them for stuffing up his hole. Tweaky *was* angry. But it served him right!

You may not believe it, but ever since Kindly taught them the trick of stuffing up their holes, the worms have done it every night. Do go and look at them some morning on the lawn, in the fields, or in the woods. You will see how cleverly they stop up their holes with all kinds of things—and they have never forgotten how to use the pine-needles properly.

"We are so nice and warm on frosty nights now," the worms say. And they are quite right. You won't forget to go and look, will you?

# The Way To The Pond

FANNY FROG has got to find
A little pond today,
She sets off merrily enough
But does she know the way?
This path or that? To left or right?
Now how is she to go?
This one may lead to Mrs. Duck,
She really doesn't know!

So will you find a way for her
That's safe right to the end,
And off she'll go with leap and bound
Round every curve and bend!

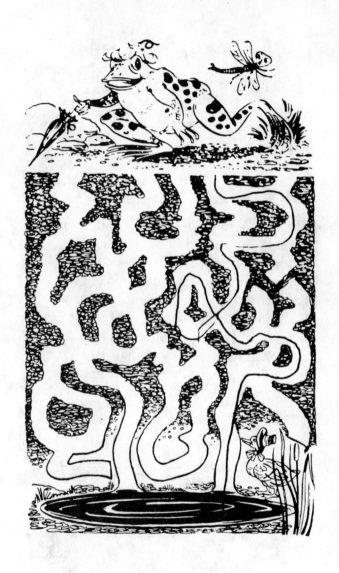

# Riddle·Me. Riddle·Me Riddle·Me·Ree

RIDDLE-ME-RIDDLE-ME, riddle-me-ree,
My first is in sugar, but not in tea,
My second's in actor, but not in stage,
My third is in chapter, but not in page,
My fourth's in gorilla, and monkey as well,
My fifth is in shout, but isn't in yell,
My last is in Lucy and Alice and Len,
But isn't in Richard or Robin or Ben,
My whole is a place that is really great fun,
And there we all go till our childhood is done!
What is it?

*(Answer on page 40)*

# The Empty Doll's House

SALLY had a lovely little doll's house on Christmas Day. She looked at it standing there at the foot of her bed. It had a little blue front door with a tiny knocker that really knocked, and it had four small windows, with tiny lace curtains at each!

"Oh, it's lovely!" said Sally. "Won't my little Belinda Jane love to live there! She is small enough to fit it properly."

But when she opened the front of the doll's house, Sally got rather a shock. It was empty. There was no furniture at all!

She was disappointed. A doll's house can't be played with unless it has furniture inside, and Sally badly wanted to play with it.

Also, Belinda Jane couldn't possibly live there if it was empty. She must at least have a bed to sleep in, a chair to sit on, and a table to have meals on.

She showed the house to Belinda Jane. Belinda looked sad when she saw that it was empty.

"Never mind. I'll save up my money and buy some furniture," said Sally. "Maybe I'll get some money today for a present."

But she didn't. All her aunts and uncles gave her Christmas presents of toys and books, and nobody gave her any money at all.

It was Granny who had given her the dear little doll's house. When she came to share Christmas dinner she spoke to Sally about the house.

"I didn't put any furniture in it, dear," she said, "because I thought you would find it more fun to buy some yourself and furnish it bit by bit."

"Yes. It *will* be fun to do that," said Sally. "Only it will take such a long time, Granny, because I spent all my money on Christmas presents, and I only get fifty pence a week, you know."

When Sally got her first fifty pence she went to the toyshop and looked at the doll's furniture there. She saw a cardboard box, and in it was a dear little bed that would just fit Belinda Jane, two chairs, a table and a wardrobe! Think of that!

But, oh dear, it cost three pounds, and there was nothing at all that fifty pence would buy! Sally ran home almost in tears!

"Now don't be a baby," said Mummy. "Everything comes to those who wait patiently. Don't get cross and upset if you can't have what you want. It will come!"

Sally was not a very patient person, and she hated waiting for things she badly wanted. But she always believed what Mummy said, so she went up to the nursery and told Belinda Jane they must both be patient, and maybe they would get the furniture somehow in the end.

Sally was excited next day, because she was going to a party—and there was to be a Christmas tree. It was sure to be a nice big one, with a present for everyone. And there would be games and balloons and crackers and ice-creams. Lovely!

She went to the party in her best blue frock. "Hallo, Sally!" cried Eileen, dancing up to her. "There's going to be a prize for every game, did you know? And it's to be money! I do hope I win a prize, because it's Mother's birthday next week, and I want to buy her some flowers."

Sally was pleased to hear about the prizes, too. If only she could win some of the money! She would be able to buy some furniture for Belinda Jane.

They played musical chairs—but Sally didn't win because a rough little boy pushed her out of her chair, and she didn't like to push back.

They played hunt the thimble, but somehow Sally never could see the thimble first! And when they played spin the trencher she couldn't get there before the little spinning tray had fallen over flat! So she didn't win any prize at all.

"Now, I mustn't get cross or upset," she said to herself. "I mustn't. I must be patient. But I've missed my chance. What a pity!"

After tea the children were taken into another room—and there was the Christmas tree, reaching up to the ceiling, hung with presents from top to bottom.

Just about the middle of the tree there hung a cardboard box—the cardboard box of furniture that Sally had seen in the toyshop! Her heart jumped for joy. Now surely her patience would have its reward—surely she would get that lovely box of doll's furniture!

She could hardly wait for the presents to be given out. She had good manners, so she didn't like to ask for the box of furniture. She just stood near by, hoping it would be hers.

But to her very great disappointment, it wasn't given to her! She was handed a box with tiny motor-cars in it instead. Sally could have cried! She said, "Thank you," and went to a corner, trying not to feel upset.

"I wanted to win a prize and I didn't. And I wanted to have the furniture off the tree and I didn't," she thought. "What's the good of being patient? I don't get what I want, however good and patient I am. I feel like shouting and stamping!"

But she didn't shout or stamp, of course, because she knew better. She just sat and looked at the little motor-cars, and didn't like them a bit.

A small girl called Fanny came up to her. She held the box of furniture in her hand. She sat down beside Sally and looked at the tiny motor-cars.

"Oh, aren't they lovely?" she said. "I do like them so much. I got this doll's furniture, look. Isn't it silly?"

"Well, I think it's lovely," said Sally. "How *can* you think it's silly?"

"It's silly for me, because I haven't got a doll's house," said Fanny. "But I *have* got a toy garage! I had it for Christmas. It's only got one car in, and I do want some more. That's why I like your present and hate mine!"

"Well, *I* had a doll's house for Christmas without any furniture—and I haven't got a garage!" said Sally, her face very bright. "Can't you give me the furniture and I'll give you the motor-cars? We could ask Eileen's mother, and see if she minds. It was she who bought all the presents for us."

They ran to Eileen's mother, and told her. She smiled at them. "Of course, change your presents if you want to," she said. "I think it would be most sensible of you. I should have given *you* the furniture, Sally, and *you* the cars, Fanny, if I'd known about the doll's house and the garage."

The little girls were so pleased. Fanny took her cars home to her toy garage and Sally raced home with her doll's furniture. It went into the doll's house and looked most beautiful!

"There you are, Belinda Jane," said Sally to her smallest doll. "Now you can move in. You've got a bed to sleep in, chairs to sit on, a wardrobe for your clothes and a table to have meals on. And I'll buy you a little cooking stove as soon as ever I can."

54

Belinda Jane was pleased. She looked sweet sitting on one of the chairs, and even sweeter tucked up in the little bed.

Mummy came to look. Sally gave her a hug. "Mummy, you were right about waiting patiently. I kept *on* being disappointed, but I wouldn't get cross or upset—and then suddenly the furniture just came to me. Wasn't it lucky?"

"It was," said Mummy. "Now, tomorrow I'll give you some old bits-and-pieces and you can make carpets for Belinda Jane. She will like that."

You should see Sally's doll's house now. She saved up her money and bought a little lamp, a cooking stove, another bed, a cupboard for the kitchen, two more chairs and a washstand. I really wouldn't mind living in that doll's house myself!

# The Boy Who Kicked

NOBODY liked to sit next to Reggie at school, because he used to kick. He thought it was funny to kick the children beside him, or behind him, too, if he could.

But they didn't think it was funny, because Reggie wore big boots, and the kicks hurt. He was a big boy for his age so nobody liked to kick him back. He could always kick much harder!

He kicked dogs if he could. The cats got out of his way quickly. If he couldn't kick anything else, he kicked stones along the road, and he was so pleased if they hit anyone!

Once he kicked his mother. But when his father heard about it, he smacked Reggie so hard that he decided he would never do that again. His father made him take off his boots, as soon as he came inside the house, for two weeks. So Reggie thought he would keep his kicks for outside. It was more fun to kick people or animals that couldn't punish him for it!

One day he went along the lane, going home from school. He came across a limping dog, and he kicked it. The dog yelped, but he couldn't run away because he had a thorn in his foot. So Reggie kicked him again.

"Stop that!" said a sharp voice, and Reggie saw a small man, not any bigger than himself, looking at him from the hedge.

"Pooh!" said Reggie, and kicked out at the dog again.

The man jumped down and held Reggie hard. Reggie kicked at the man's ankles and made him yell. "You let me go!" said Reggie.

"I don't believe you're a boy at all," said the man. "I believe you're a little donkey, who has been changed by a spell into a little boy. Poor thing! I'm sorry for you."

Reggie kicked at a flower and its head flew off. "Don't be silly," he said to the man.

"I'll change you back to a donkey," said the man. "I've often changed people back to their own shape when witches or wizards had turned them into something. And I can easily turn you back into yourself, poor little kicking donkey."

And before Reggie knew what was happening, the little man was drawing a circle in white chalk round him, and was chanting some very queer words indeed.

When he had finished, there was no Reggie there. Instead there was a nice little grey donkey, with long ears and tail that switched from side to side.

"There!" said the little man, and patted the donkey. "You're back to your own shape, little kicker. You will be happy now. Donkeys always kick and people expect them to. But not little boys."

58

Reggie was so angry that he kicked out with his hind legs at once. But the little man skipped out of the way. "Good little donkey!" he said. "Good little kicker!"

Reggie went slowly home, angry and frightened. He found himself munching grass and thistles. *Thistles*! He didn't want to eat them at all, but he had to, because he was a donkey.

A man came up to him. "Where are you straying from?" he asked. "You'd better come with me. You must belong to the farmer near by."

Reggie kicked out at once, because he didn't like the man. "Oho!" said the fellow at once. "Bad-tempered, are you! Well, I've a cure for that!" And he brought his stick down so sharply on Reggie's back that he hee-hawed loudly in pain.

"You can kick all you like," said the man. "But each time you do, you'll feel my stick!"

Reggie broke away from him and trotted home. His mother was amazed to see a little grey donkey putting his head round the kitchen door. "Go away!" she said. "Do you belong to the milkman? Go away."

It was dreadful to have his own mother telling him to go away. The milkman came just them and Reggie's mother asked him to take the donkey out to the lane. "He must have wandered away from somewhere," she said.

Reggie didn't want to go. He kicked out at the milkman. The man, who was used to donkeys,

59

gave him a sharp slap. "A kicker, are you?" he
said. "Well, kickers are no use to anyone. Out you
go!"

Into the lane went poor Reggie, and the
milkman slammed the gate shut so that he could
not go in to see his mother again.

He spent the whole night out, and he didn't like
it a bit. In the morning, the little magic man came
up to him again.

"I say!" he said. "I find I've made a mistake.
You really *ought* to be a little boy, not a donkey.
But you can't blame me for my mistake, because of
your kicking. I'd better change you back."

"Please do," hee-hawed Reggie.

60

"Well, I will—but be careful you don't get changed into a donkey by one of my friends, if you start kicking again," said the little fellow. "They'll think the same as I did—that you're a poor little donkey changed by a witch into a nasty little boy!"

Once more the chalk circle was drawn round Reggie, and the magic words chanted. Then, hey presto! he was himself again, with no long ears to twitch, nor long tail to swing. How glad he was!

His father was angry with him for staying out all night, and wouldn't believe him when he told him what had happened. "If I have any more nonsense from you, Reggie, I shall take my slipper and spank you for five minutes," said he. "How would you like that?"

Reggie knew he wouldn't like it at all, so he said nothing. He didn't even want to kick! He didn't feel like a kicking donkey any more, and never would.

Now it's quite safe to sit next to Reggie at school, and not even the slowest old dog is afraid of him. It's a good thing that little man found out his mistake, or Reggie would still be in a field somewhere, munching prickly thistles!